AF580537

for Rafiki

front & back cover art
courtesy of Allan Swart/Pixels.com
used by permission

THE GOOD FIGHT

screenplay by

Mark Heath Howard

DING! DING!

SMASH IN:

INT. ARENA - BOXING RING - NIGHT

SUPERIMPOSED: *Grand vs Presley - Las Vegas, Nevada*

AUDIENCE is thunderous!

Two heavyweights go at it! The #1 contender, TIMOTHY "PRECISION" PRESLEY (30s), a light-skinned African American with a very non-threatening look, struggles to cover his bruised ribs and bleeding right eye! The #2 contender, AMOR "DA BOTTOM" GRAND (30s), brandishing Miami-style dreadlocks and gold teeth with dark brown skin, spews taunts and rebellious smiles!

GRAND
(maniacal)
Say it! SAY IT!

The pre-bell *CLICKING* distracts Grand. He's rocked by Presley's straight right! Grand clutches.

BELL!

Grand looks out over the ropes. He searches FACES. He sits on the stool. There's something unsettling in his eyes. PAUL "SWEET PEA" LORDE (60s), African American, Grand's trainer, looks at his fighter long and hard.

SWEET PEA
What the hell was that?

COMMENTATOR #1
This'll be another social media gem!

COMMENTATOR #2
If Grand is not careful, "Precision" might give us something to talk about!

COMMENTATOR #3
Trash talk or not, "The Bottom" has certainly done significant damage downstairs.

SWEET PEA
We not doing this again. He's gone. Focus on Presley and end this!

Grand seems to snap out of his fog. His eyes lock on Presley.

SWEET PEA (CONT'D)
There we go.

JUMPCUT - MOMENTS LATER

Grand is at it again--trashtalking and showboating!

SWEET PEA
GRAND!

GRAND
I got this, Pea. This nigga-

Presley whips a precise combo! He drops Grand!

COMMENTATOR #3
Down goes Grand!

REFEREE (40s) pushes Presley away!

PRESLEY
(mockingly)
"The Bottom".

COMMENTATOR #1
"#thebottom"!

REFEREE
(over Grand)
ONE...TWO...THREE...

SWEET PEA
FOR REAL!?

Sweet Pea's about to throw in the towel!

REFEREE
(continuing)
...FOUR...FIVE...

Grand rests his gloves on his forehead. Smiling. He throws a wink to the commentators. Sweet Pea drops his head in his hands. Grand sits up. Stares at Presley.

GRAND
What number you on, Ref?

REFEREE
(continuing)
...SIX...SEVEN...EIGHT...

Grand rises to his feet.

GRAND
I'm up. I'm good.
(to Presley)
That tickled.

REFEREE
Gimme your hands. Look at me. You good?

GRAND
Nigga! Ain't that what I just said!? Move.

REFEREE
Keep it clean, Grand.

Referee rejoins them. Presley keeps mocking. Grand drops his guard.

SWEET PEA
WHAT THE...!? Pick up your hands!

Grand leans in. Taunts. Presley throws a malicious punch! Grand ducks and smashes a bone-cracking body shot! Presley drops to one knee! Spits out his mouthpiece!

GRAND
That's "Da Bottom", mothafucka!

PRESLEY
(shouts back)
Like your crackhead daddy! He ain't come up and you won't either!

Sweet Pea sees it coming!

SWEET PEA
No, Amor!

Grand crushes Presley with one punch!

BELL RINGS!!!!!!!

Mayhem explodes as Grand tries to fight off PRESLEY'S CORNER, BOXING OFFICIALS and POLICE OFFICERS!

INT. SWEET PEA'S HOME - OFFICE - NIGHT

Sweet Pea and TED STURGE (50s), Caucasian American, talk. Ted's a powerful person within a small circle boxing royalty. The friendship goes way back.

SWEET PEA
He's sensitive about his ol' man. May he rest in peace. Presley hit low. You remember Cooney and Holmes?

TED
Your boy's a grown man. He's in the ring, not his father. Besides, Presley clearly was on one knee with his glove on the canvas.

SWEET PEA
It wasn't...uh...malicious. Knee-jerk reaction. Like a...uh...counter-punch.

TED
Sorry. That's disqualification. Anywhere.

SWEET PEA
And seventy-five percent of his purse with a suspension?

TED
Grand knew the consequences before he laced up.

SWEET PEA
What about forgiveness? Absolution?

TED
You're the saint, Paul. Not the SAC.

SWEET PEA
Ted, he's gonna need the money.

TED
How's he doing?
(off Sweet Pea's silence)
Well, it's outta my hands, Paul. Millions of people and three judges all saw the same thing.

SWEET PEA
And how many millions do you think still wanna see the champ, Dane, versus Amor "Da Bottom" Grand?

TED
(gets up to leave)
Well, you got a point. But-

SWEET PEA
(stops Ted)
-Look, Ted, I'm the first one in Amor's face about his issues, but the bottom line is-

Grand storms in--face still swollen from the fight.

GRAND
-"Da Bottom" fills the seats. That's the bottom line...Mr. Sturge. The Legend.

Ted shows a subtle smile.

INT. SWEET PEA'S HOME - DEN - DAY

Grand sits sunken in a leather recliner with shades on. A mean scowl wipes away the smile.

PRESLEY
(on tv)
Grand's a thug. He didn't win. This is boxing, not street-fightin'. This ain't the gutter. Guess that's why he's "Da Bottom". Fits him. He shoulda tattoo'd it across his stomach.

SWEET PEA
(entering with drinks)
Turn that off. I said to never watch the news after a loss.

Grand turns the tv off. Sweet Pea puts drinks down.

GRAND
(sips)
Uh oh. You serving tea. What he say?

SWEET PEA
Eirene still a praying woman?

GRAND
(diappointedly matter-of-fact)
I need a miracle.

SWEET PEA
To square off with Dane, you do.

Grand checks his cellphone: "*CREDITOR*".

SWEET PEA (CONT'D)
Talk to Him.

INT. GRAND'S CAR - DAY

Grand pulls up to a red light in a CONVERTIBLE BENZ. He attracts a PANHANDLER (50s), Caucasian American, who realizes he's in the presence of money.

PANHANDLER
C'mon dude. I know you got it. Help a brother out.

Panhandler taps on the makeshift sign. Shakes a plastic cup full of coins. Agitated, Grand pushes the button to close the convertible. Green light. He drives off!

EXT. GRAND'S APARTMENT - DAY

Grand has his cellphone in hand. He snatches down an eviction notice!

VOICEMAIL MESSAGE
Hello, this message is for Amor Grand. This is United Credit Assistance calling about your 2018 Mercedes Benz. Please-

Grand slams the door behind him!

INT. GRAND'S APARTMENT - DAY

Grand rips the notice! Clutter. Stacks of bill envelopes. He drops into the couch. Flips through messages on his cell-phone.

EXT. GRAND'S APARTMENT - CONTINUOUS

A tow truck hooks up and pulls off with Grand's Benz. Too late, Grand storms out!

GRAND
HEY! I'M AMOR "DA BOTTOM" GRAND! HEY!

Grand's chase cannot catch up with the tow truck.

INT. GRAND'S APARTMENT - DAY

Grand answers his ringing cellphone. EIRENE GRAND (60s), African American, wants facetime.

GRAND
(beat)
Hey Mama.

EIRENE
Morrie? You okay? What's this I hear, you hit somebody while they were on their knees praying?

GRAND
No Mama. Did you watch--You didn't watch my fight.

EIRENE
Not even King David touched a man while he was praying. You don't do that, Morrie. I raised you better than that. Lord, if only your father was-

GRAND
-Mama.
(beat)
May I please call you back?

EIRENE
Okay, baby. But you remember God still loves you and He wants to talk with you. You can come back home. You know that, right?

GRAND
Yes, Mama.

EIRENE
I'll be praying for you. Bye son.

GRAND
Bye Mama.

Grand belts out a yowl! Silence. Phone rings.

EXT. HOMELESS SHELTER - DAY

Grand exits a RIDESHARE CAR. A frown blankets his face. Passing a line of homeless MEN, WOMEN and CHILDREN, MEDIA swarms.

REPORTER #1
Grand, will you be ready for the champ, Roc Dane?

REPORTER #2
Is this a financial or professional decision?

REPORTER #3
Was it Dane's words about your father? Is it personal?

SWEET PEA
(walking up)
Welcome to your miracle.

Sweet Pea slaps an apron, gloves and a plastic cap into Grand's chest and pulls him through.

INT. HOMELESS SHELTER - DAY

Grand is on the serving line. He notices NYLA HARRIS (30s), African American, going throughout greeting and serving. Their eyes meet. She heads straight for him.

SWEET PEA
(aside to Grand)
That's the woman in charge. Miss Harris.

NYLA
Name?

GRAND
You playing, right?

SWEET PEA
She don't feint.

GRAND
I'm Amor "Da Bottom" Grand. The number one contend-

NYLA
(sticks nametag to his shirt)
-"Mr. Bottom".

GRAND
Call me Grand.

NYLA
(continuing)
The pass you've been given today in exchange to do what you do is not to be taken for granted. You're a servant now. This is where you really fight for the people.

She fills the passing trays with a fixed smile, nudges him and returns to the tables.

GRAND
Thanks for your help.

NYLA
My pleasure. "Grand".

Grand smiles.

INT. HOMELESS SHELTER - KITCHEN - LATER

Grand half-washes dishes. He peeks through the door window. Reporters stick microphones, cellphones and cameras in Sweet Pea's face.

SWEET PEA
My fighter has taken full responsibility for his...past unfortunate act in the ring. My thanks to the SAC for a swift and fair penalty and opportunity. Next, my fighter will begin his preparation for a chance to be the heavyweight champ of the world.

Grand cues up sports news on his cellphone: *SOUND BITES* and FOOTAGE of Grand's troubled past.

ANALYST #1
(from cellphone)
As much bad press that comes with Grand, he's a draw. A popular fighter. People wanna see him. This fight? Most likely, a "go". Money drives the sport of boxing now. Not the fighters.

ANALYST #2
"Street-fighter" according to Precision Presley.

Laughter.

ANALYST #3
I got three letters and a word, guys: FTX. Arena.

ANALYSTS
WHOOOOOOA!

Nyla comes from a back office. Grand rushes to the sink. He drops his phone. Nyla picks it up. Grand takes it from her.

NYLA
Don't worry. I'm not a judge.

Grand blocks Nyla from the door.

GRAND
That depends on what you know.

NYLA
Right. And I don't know you.

GRAND
Nice counter. That's wassup.
(holds out his hand)
Amor Grand, remember?

NYLA
(shakes his hand)
Nyla Harris. Officially. Why "da bottom"?

GRAND
I'm from Miami.

NYLA
Oh. Right. "The bottom". Mr. Bottom.
(smiles)
Grand, I'm appreciative that you agreed to do this--whether reluctantly or not--but there are no flashing lights and round girls sashaying through here.

GRAND
Yo, I-

NYLA
-And no cameras.

GRAND
Yo. Look. I'm here. The reporters ain't-

NYLA
-Would you be here if you didn't have to?
(off Grand's silence)
That's what I thought.

GRAND
Hey, I ain't on another planet. I know the struggle.
(their eyes connect)
No caps.

NYLA
Okay.

GRAND
You like fights?

NYLA
Only if I win.

GRAND
Oh, the counter. Lemme invite you to one.

NYLA
You don't even know me.

GRAND
I know you got a heart for the people. And Pea said you put this together.

NYLA
"This"? We feed, house and educate people here. Tonight, potentially, in the US, more than half a million people could experience homelessness. My prayer is that number decreases. That's what I fight for.

GRAND
That counter.
(off Nyla's smile)
So, you down?

NYLA
What makes you think I wanna...when

NYLA (CONT'D)
is this fight?

GRAND
I don't know. Pea got that.

NYLA
Is it yours?

GRAND
Yep.

NYLA
Where?
(off Grand's playful shrug)
How about I just pray for you?

GRAND
I ain't no charity case.

NYLA
Not receptive? A'ight then.

SWEET PEA'S VOICE (OS)
Amor. Amor!? Where are you?

GRAND
The kitchen, Pea.

Sweet Pea pushes in fast! Elated!

GRAND (CONT'D)
Pea, me and my invited guest, Nyla Harris, were just talking about-

SWEET PEA
-The fight!?
(to Nyla)
Miss Harris, you like sunny beaches?

GRAND
WHAT!? TRUE THAT!

Thrilled, Grand picks up Nyla! Surprised, she likes it.

EXT. GRAND'S APARTMENT - DAYS LATER

RIDESHARE CAR pulls up to more NEWS REPORTERS! They pounce! All of Grand's belongings are on the sidewalk and street!

INT. FTX ARENA - BOXING RING - NIGHT

SUPERIMPOSED: *Grand vs Dane - Heavyweight Title - Miami, FL*

The champion, ROC DANE (30s), African American, taller and heavier, meets Grand center ring and goes right at him with two hooks to the body and a hard uppercut! Grand stumbles, hurt, with blood spilling down his nose! He grabs tight!

SWEET PEA
Leave him with somethin'!

Grand lets off two quick hooks to the body of his own and a hook upstairs! He backs away. Dane resumes the charge!

NYLA
(near ringside)
Hit him again! Don't back up!

SWEET PEA
Keep him off ya with the jab, Amor.
(Grand retreats)
The jab! Not your feet! Stop runnin'!

Dane cuts off Grand! Grand sticks in a couple jabs for space! Dane ducks and slides and lands a straight right! Grand counters with a wicked left hook! They circle and faint. Grand backs again. Dane shrinks the ring! He corners Grand!

NYLA
Stop backing up! Get outta there!

Grand blocks, but Dane unloads!

SWEET PEA
Roll out!

Grand, Mayweather-like, shoulder rolls, and tattoos Dane with a three-punch combo! Dane counters! They lock up. Referee separates. *CLICKING* cue causes Grand to flinch and frown again.

DING! End of ROUND 5.

DANE
(passing Grand)
Your daddy was garbage.

Grand backs to his corner. His eyes burn into Dane's back. Sweet Pea springs into the ring and watches Grand closely.

SWEET PEA
Let that go.

GRAND
Fuck that! You heard what he said!?

SWEET PEA
I'm talking about the bell cue.

Grand looks hard at Sweet Pea. Sweet Pea takes out Grand's mouthpiece. FREDDY STACKS (50s), Caucasian American, wipes Grand's face before he sticks swabs up Grand's nose. TINY JONES (60s), African American, squirts water. Grand spits.

SWEET PEA (CONT'D)
Stop running. Your legs gonna give out before the 12th.

GRAND
We ain't going that far. Hit me again, Tiny.

Grand snatches the water from Tiny.

FREDDY
You ain't quittin' is ya, AG?

GRAND
(steals a glance at Nyla)
"Quit"? Freddy, you gon' get these hands too. Time to get paid. Mouthpiece!

DING! Start of ROUND 6.

NYLA
Only forward, Grand!

GRAND
Whatchu said about my daddy?
(lands a jab)
Huh?
(lands a combo)
I can't hear you!

TINY
Oh Lord. He at it again.

SWEET PEA
Grand, listen to me! <u>Shut</u>! <u>Up</u>!

FREDDY
Just fight, AG.

GRAND
That's all I do.

Grand hurts Dane with a head and body shot! He rocks the champ with a vicious uppercut! Dane bounces back from off the ropes as Grand tags him with a flurry of shots!

SWEET PEA
Do it! Knock him out!

CROWD
DA BOTTOM! DA BOTTOM!

Grand folds Dane with a devastating kidney shot! Dane drops to his knees!

SWEET PEA
(off Grand's wind up)
NO NO NO NO NO NO NO!

Grand puts the brakes on any disqualifying punches. He throws Sweet Pea a wink instead.

GRAND
(to Dane)
<u>Former</u> champ. Garbage.

Dane is counted out. It's over!

DING! DING! DING!

Grand raises his hands and rushes to the neutral corner! Climbs the ropes and points out!

<u>INT. BOXING RING - LATER</u>

With Sweet Pea on his left, Nyla on his right and the heavyweight belt on his shoulder, Grand snatches the microphone and steals the spotlight.

GRAND
This for you, Miami! For Liberty City!
"Da bottom", baby! "Da bottom"!

He drops the mic! Kisses Nyla!

EXT. FANCY RESTAURANT - NIGHT

Nyla pushes through the door and stops on the sidewalk. No smile. Her arms are folded. Grand strolls behind taking selfies and flirts with FANS. VALET (20s) is apprehensive.

VALET
Uh...ticket, Mr. Grand?

GRAND
Don't you see I'm busy?

Nyla takes out her phone and clicks on a rideshare app.

NYLA
Will you give him the ticket so we can go!? Or do I need to-

GRAND
(hands over the ticket)
-Relax? Yes. You do.

NYLA
Excuse me?

Nyla stares him down. Grand steps away from the fans.

GRAND
That's it yaw'll.

FAN
Just one more?

GRAND
(snaps)
I said that's it!

Fans murmur and disperse. Valet pulls the ESCALADE TRUCK up. Nyla gets in. Grand tips.

INT. ESCALADE TRUCK - NIGHT

Grand pulls off. Slams on the brakes! Panhandler walks in front with his plastic cup full of coins.

FLASHBACK - EXT. STORAGE FACILITY - DAY

Grand hides his face as he hauls his belongings off a moving truck. MAN (40s) approaches.

MAN
Hey, aren't you-

GRAND
-I don't need help. I'm good.

MAN
But-

GRAND
-I said I'm good.

INT. ESCALADE TRUCK - PRESENT NIGHT

The panhandler shakes the plastic cup of coins! Grand is pissed at its sound!

GRAND
(lays on the horn)
MOVE!

Grand swerves past and speeds away! Nyla burns her eyes into his face!

NYLA
Take me home.

Grand scowls at her--trying to shake the growing pain in his head.

INT. GRAND'S MANSION - LIVINGROOM - NIGHT

On the floor, staring up at the ceiling, Grand ignores his ringing cellphone. He pops a couple aspirins. The furnishing is sparse.

FLASHBACK - INT. MOTEL LOBBY - NIGHT

Grand frowns on the up-keeping. The place is rundown. He wears a cap and shades. PATRONS appear as if they have just walked in off the streets.

INT. BOXING GYM - PRESENT DAY

With earplugs jammed in, Grand works the speed bag!

SWEET PEA
(makes himself visible)
Amor. Amor. Champ! You lied to me?

Grand roars through his last punch!

DREAM SEQUENCE - INT. RENTAL CAR - NIGHT

Grand gets in with rental papers. He quickly reviews the price and rental length. Grand hears something. A smacking sound increases!

MALE SILHOUETTE emerges in the back seat.

MAN'S VOICE
How long you stayin' here?

INT. GRAND'S MANSION - LIVINGROOM - PRESENT NIGHT

Grand is jolted out of his sleep! Still on the floor, he grabs his aching back.

Cellphone *RINGS*. He smiles when he sees it.

EXT. GRAND'S MANSION - NIGHT

Nyla and Grand sit on a swinging bench on the porch.

GRAND
Wassup?

NYLA
I wanna...I wanna ask you something.

GRAND
Okay. You don't wanna talk inside?

NYLA
No. This is fine. Please?

GRAND
Cool.

NYLA
I wanna tell you something, too.
Something I need to do.

GRAND
I'm listening.

NYLA
But, I need you to do something no matter what your answer is to my question. Because, regardless, I'm still gonna do what I need to do.

Grand's face twists with confusion. Nyla nervously giggles.

NYLA (CONT'D)
(beat)
Are you saved?

GRAND
(beat)
Um...huh?

NYLA
"Saved". Are you? Do you-

GRAND
-Go to church? Believe in God?

NYLA
That's part of it. I'm asking if you've received Jesus Christ as your personal Lord and Savior.
(he looks away)
Grand?

GRAND
I did. My mama, she...Long time ago. But...
(he shifts)
...me and God ain't talked in awhile. Amor "Da Backslider" Grand.

NYLA
I'm not judging you. I just wanted to know. I prayed about it and the Holy Spirit said, "Ask him".

GRAND
Okay. That's your question. Now what you need to tell me? Get ready? Jesus comin' soon?

NYLA
(laughs lightly)
No. But if you wanna repent, we can pray-

GRAND
-I'm good.

Nyla senses his shift. She takes his hand. Looks him straight in the eyes.

NYLA
I think we need to put things on hold. Slow down.

GRAND
What!?

NYLA
I believe we're unequally yoked. And I can't...I won't go any further...

GRAND
You What!?
(aside)
I ain't even hit it yet.

NYLA
(obliviously continues)
...For me, if a relationship was to begin, we both need to be in right fellowship with God. And if you-

GRAND
-ME!?

NYLA
Grand, please don't raise your voice.

GRAND
You could've phoned this in! Hell, text'd it!

NYLA
Lower your voice or I will get in my car and-

INT. GRAND'S MANSION - LIVINGROOM - MOMENTS LATER

Grand slams the door! He turns and punches a hole in the wall!

GRAND
ARGHHHHHHHHHHHHHHHHHHH!

FLASHBACK - EXT. WOMAN'S APARTMENT - DAY

WOMAN (20s), African American, pushes Grand OUT!

GRAND
Baby, where I'ma go?

WOMAN
"Baby"? Nigga, I don't care where you go, but you ain't staying here!

She slams the door in his face! Grand walks and shatters a car window with one punch!

INT. BOXING GYM - PRESENT DAY

Grand beelines directly to Sweet Pea who's focused on the training action and other BOXERS.

GRAND
I'm ready.

SWEET PEA
(without missing a beat)
Change. Get wrapped. Warm up. Lace 'em. And show me that sweet science.

GRAND
Not that, Pea.

SWEET PEA
Grand, there's nothing but that. <u>This</u>.

GRAND
I'm ready to talk. To Ceasar.

Sweet Pea's blind-sided. He drops his head--ignoring what's inside the ring. Eternity passes before he looks to Grand.

INT. SUBSTANCE ABUSE COUNSELOR'S OFFICE - DAY

COUNSELOR (40s), African American, sits across from an empty chair. He writes on a clipboard and looks over the top of thin-rimmed glasses. Grand stands against the wall. He's just about had it.

WE HEAR incessant throat clearing and coughing. CEASAR GRAND (60s), African American, a shell of a man, sits in a chair facing the counselor. He occasionally fidgets and twitches.

CEASAR
Yep. TD. Drugs didn't help. Prescription. Illegal. No help. My son. Grand. He the champ. I'm proud of him.

Beat. Grand comes off the wall. Lingers. Sits.

GRAND
(finally looks at Ceasar)
Why you here?

COUNSELOR
Grand, your father, Ceasar-

GRAND
-Why you keep saying our names like we don't know each other!? I wanna know why he here! "He the champ. I'm proud of you", that's supposed to make up for years of abuse and neglect!? Huh!?

COUNSELOR
Grand. Relax.

Grand frowns again at the *CLICKING*.

CEASAR
Why you here?

GRAND
(audacious laugh)
What!? Nigga! You asked me to come!

CEASAR
You still angry at me. Why come? If you still angry.

Grand is stumped.

GRAND
My mama said you wanted to see me.

Ceasar goes completely quiet. He lowers his head. Closes his eyes.

CEASAR
Ain't talk to Eirene. Been twenty years. Pretty Reney. Can't find no good memories.

FLASHBACK - INT. APARTMENT - NIGHT

EIRENE GRAND, 40s, clutches AMOR GRAND, 10, for dear life. CEASAR GRAND, 40s, is maniacal! He shouts, yells, screams, smashes, destroys and even shadow-boxes as he demands!

CEASAR
WHERE MY MONEY, RENEY!? WHERE IT AT!? YOU HID IT! WHERE IT AT!?

EIRENE
Just leave Ceasar or I'm calling the police again! Please! Just GO!
(aside)
Oh God, please help him. Help him Lord. Please.

Grand has tears in his eyes.

INT. SUBSTANCE ABUSE COUNSELOR'S OFFICE - PRESENT DAY

GRAND
(choking up)
Liar! I saw you. Again. And again. And again.

CEASAR
Last time I saw your mama. Pretty Reney. Alleys by your school. The park. Streets. Behind the gym. Stoplights. Never that house after that. My home. No roof.

GRAND
Why you ain't come back, man!? Why you ain't try to work it out!? What about Mama!? Us!? Me!? You left us! You left me!

Counselor slowly walks beside Grand.

CEASAR
Reney. Your mama. She wanted God to help. I wanted to fix myself. By myself. Do it alone. That's how I failed at it.

Grand flips his chair across the room! Counselor waves off SECURITY outside the door. Ceasar gets up, gingerly. He walks over to Grand. Grand flexes to strike. He doesn't.

CEASAR (CONT'D)
Grand. My son. The Champ. I'm sorry. I'm sorry.

Ceasar puts his arms around Grand. Grand bawls and hugs him back.

INT. CHURCH - BAPTISM POOL - DAY

With Sweet Pea, Eirene and Nyla in the CONGREGATION, they watch the TWO DEACONS (50s) help Grand into the water.

DEACON #1
Amor Grand, on the profession of your faith in the Lord Jesus Christ that he died on the cross and God raised Him from the dead, I now baptize you in the name of the Father, the Son and the Holy Ghost.

Grand is submerged under water! Brought back up!

INT. CHURCH - SANCTUARY - LATER

Grand emerges dry, in a sharp dark suit. Nyla runs and hugs him. Grand kisses Eirene. Shakes Sweet Pea's hand.

SWEET PEA
(aside)
Did you repent about lying to me about your father?

EIRENE
We're in your corner, Morrie.

GRAND
Thanks Mama. I felt like yaw'll was in the water with me.

EIRENE
Baby, Mama got her own tub at home. I was with you in spirit.

GRAND
That's what I--nevermind, Mama.

INT. CHAMPIONS REFUGE FACILITY - DAY

SUPERIMPOSED: *One Year Later*

With a sincere smile and a wedding band on his finger, Grand has on gloves, an apron and a plastic cap. He fills the passing trays for MEN, WOMEN and CHILDREN.

NYLA
Grand, someone wanted to take a picture with the champ.

GRAND
That's former champ. I'm retired, remember.

NYLA
Baby, you know you always my champ.

GRAND
That counter.

Pregnant, and proudly admiring the huge rock on her finger, Nyla steps aside. The plastic cup-shaking panhandler appears. The three stand with fixed smiles as a SERVER readies the cellphone.

PANHANDLER
Mr. Champ.

GRAND
Call me Grand.
(holds out his hand)
What's your name, sir?

PANHANDLER
(shakes his hand)
Frank.

GRAND
Nice to meet you, Frank.

They huddle for the picture.

NYLA
Grand, you got a new phone?

GRAND
No. I thought it was yours.

NYLA
Not mine.

GRAND
Whose is it?

Panhandler shakes the plastic cup of coins.

SERVER
Say "champions".

Nyla and the panhandler smile. Grand's face contorts. FREEZE FRAME!

BLACK OUT.

www.ingramcontent.com/pod-product-compliance
Lightning Source LLC
LaVergne TN
LVHW080559160826
845677LV00010B/1918
9798355596323